The Burglar's Breakfast

Felicity Everett

Adapted by Lesley Sims

Illustrated by Christyan Fox

Reading Consultant: Alison Kelly
Roehampton University

Contents

Chapter 1

Breakfast!

Alfie Briggs was a burglar.
But he wasn't a good one.
Tonight, he'd stolen a broken
lawn mower and a bird...

...a talking bird. It almost woke up the whole street.

After a hard night, Alfie liked to go home to a tasty breakfast.

Breakfast was his main meal of the day. He always ate at least three courses.

He tried to
make sure he never
ran out of the five
breakfast foods
he liked best.

Looking around his kitchen, it was easy to see what they were.

7

Chapter 2

No breakfast...

Alfie's stomach
gave a hungry
growl. It was time
for breakfast.

Mmm.
What shall I have
first? Cornflakes
I think.

He hunted high...

8

...and low. But he couldn't find the cornflakes.

Just then, he noticed a
trail of cornflakes leading
out of the door...

...and up the street. It could
only mean one thing.

Someone had stolen Alfie's cornflakes.

He decided to track down the thief and get back his breakfast.

Chapter 3

On the trail

Nose pressed against his magnifying glass, Alfie followed the cornflake trail.

He followed the trail into
the park. He followed it to
Pets' Corner. The thief would
be sorry he'd stolen from Alfie.

13

Suddenly, Alfie came face to face with the thief. The thief looked even grumpier than Alfie. What's more, he had two sharp horns.

"Er, nice goat!" said Alfie.
The goat glared. Perhaps he
didn't like having his
breakfast interrupted.

On his way home,
Alfie thought about what
he'd have for breakfast
instead of cornflakes.

Scrambled egg.
Nice and runny with
lots of butter.

Feeling happier, he strode
along when ⟨crunch!⟩ Alfie
stepped on a broken egg shell
beside the hedge.

"Someone else has had
the same idea!" he said
and grinned.
He thought he knew who
that someone was.

Alfie knelt down. He
crawled through a hole in the
hedge. On the other side were
more broken shells and
one happy fox.

The fox ran off. Alfie
spotted something.

Alfie was cross. First, his cornflakes had been snaffled by a greedy goat. Now his plan for eggs had been scrambled by a cheeky fox.

He stomped home. He flung open his front door. Then he stormed into the kitchen.

Chapter 4

Cat and mouse

"Right," Alfie said, crossly. "It will have to be sardines. Now, where did I put them... Huh?"

He was staring at an empty plate. All six sardines had vanished. But this time, he had a good idea who the thief was.

TIBBLES! Keep your thieving paws to yourself.

Alfie was furious. First, no cornflakes. Then, no eggs. Now, no sardines. He would have to make waffles.

24

Alfie set the table and
turned on the oven. Then
he went to get
his waffles.

Grrr! Someone had beaten
him to it. Luckily, they'd left
a trail. Alfie followed it.

The thieves hadn't eaten
the waffles. But now Alfie
didn't want to eat them either.

27

Chapter 5

Sugar shock

Alfie sighed. No cornflakes, no eggs, no sardines, no waffles. Was there anything to eat?

He was in luck. There was
a big juicy grapefruit in the
fruit bowl.

"Mmm, lovely," said Alfie.
He licked his lips. "I'll just
get the sugar..."

It wasn't just one sneaky creep. There were hundreds.
But they were very small.

Alfie took out his magnifying glass. He'd soon find out who was making off with his sugar.

31

Chapter 6

Still no breakfast

By the time Alfie had solved
the mystery, there wasn't a
single grain of sugar left.

Alfie felt hungry and very,
very cross.

"No cornflakes, no eggs, no sardines, no waffles!" he yelled. A few seconds later, he had no grapefruit either.

Then he paused. Oh dear!
Maybe this was how people
felt when he burgled their
houses. Alfie felt ashamed.

But he also still felt hungry.
There was only one thing left
to do. He would have to go
out for breakfast.

Chapter 7

Paper plan

At Rosie's Café, Alfie ate an enormous breakfast. But even that didn't cheer him up.

I don't want to be a burglar any more. But what else can I do?

As he drank his coffee, Alfie glanced at a newspaper. He read something which gave him an idea.

He took a closer look.

NEED A JOB?

Can you:
Follow trails?
Track down stolen goods?
Catch crooks?
Spot clues?
Keep a cool head?

The STOP-A-THIEF
Detective Agency
needs
YOU!

"Can I follow trails?"
thought Alfie, remembering
his trip to the park.

"Can I track down stolen goods?" he wondered.

"Without even trying!" he said.

40

"Can I catch crooks?" he asked himself. "I certainly can – and Tibbles won't steal my fish again!"

"Can I spot clues?" he said.
He rubbed his chin. "Ha! I
can spot clues almost invisible
to the naked eye."

Chapter 8

A new job?

"I can do all of those things!" said Alfie. Then he read the last line of the list.

"Can I keep a cool head? Hmmm..."

Alfie shrugged. He hadn't
been cool about the grapefruit.
But who can keep their cool
when they're very hungry?

The Stop-A-Thief Detective
Agency gave Alfie a job the
same day. The boss had never
known anyone like him.

45

Alfie caught more crooks in his first week than all the other detectives put together.

And he never stole another thing – not even breakfast.

Try these other books in
Series One:

The Dinosaurs Next Door: Stan
loves living next door to Mr. Puff.
His house is full of amazing things.
Best of all are the dinosaur eggs —
until they begin to hatch...

The Monster Gang: Starting a
gang is a great idea. So is dressing
up like monsters. But if everyone
is in disguise, how do you know
who's who?

Designed by
Amanda Gulliver,
Katarina Dragoslavic
and Maria Wheatley

This edition first published in 2007 by Usborne Publishing Ltd.,
Usborne House, 83-85 Saffron Hill, London EC1N 8RT, England.
www.usborne.com
Copyright © 2007, 2002, 1996, 1995 Usborne Publishing Ltd.

48